A NOTE TO PARENTS

Reading Aloud with Your Child

Research shows that reading books aloud is the single most valuable support parents can provide in helping children learn to read.

- Be a ham! The more enthusiasm you display, the more your child will enjoy the book.
- Run your finger underneath the words as you read to signal that the print carries the story.
- Leave time for examining the illustrations more closely; encourage your child to find things in the pictures.
- Invite your youngster to join in whenever there's a repeated phrase in the text.
- Link up events in the book with similar events in your child's life.
- If your child asks a question, stop and answer it. The book can be a means to learning more about your child's thoughts.

Listening to Your Child Read Aloud

The support of your attention and praise is absolutely crucial to your child's continuing efforts to learn to read.

- If your child is learning to read and asks for a word, give it immediately so that the meaning of the story is not interrupted. DO NOT ask your child to sound out the word.
- On the other hand, if your child initiates the act of sounding out, don't intervene.
- If your child is reading along and makes what is called a miscue, listen for the sense of the miscue. If the word "road" is substituted for the word "street," for instance, no meaning is lost. Don't stop the reading for a correction.
- If the miscue makes no sense (for example, "horse" for "house"), ask your child to reread the sentence because you're not sure you understand what's just been read.
- Above all else, enjoy your child's growing command of print and make sure you give lots of praise. *You are your child's first teacher — and the most important one. Praise from you is critical for further risk-taking and learning.*

— Priscilla Lynch
Ph.D., New York University
Educational Consultant

To the new boys—
Nicholas, Adrian, Conor, Jackson,
Jesse, Oliver, and Teddy
—J.P.

Text copyright © 1994 by James Preller.
Illustrations copyright © 1994 by Hans Wilhelm Inc.
All rights reserved. Published by Scholastic Inc.
HELLO READER! and CARTWHEEL BOOKS are registered trademarks
of Scholastic Inc.

Library of Congress Cataloging-in-Publication Data

Preller, James.
Hiccups for Elephant / by James Preller : illustrated by Hans Wilhelm.
p.   cm. — (Hello reader! Level 2)
ISBN 0-590-48588-1
[1. Hiccups—Fiction. 2. Elephants—Fiction. 3. Animals—Fiction.
4. Sleep—Fiction.] I. Wilhelm, Hans, 1945-
ill. II. Title. III. Series.
PZ7.P915Hi   1994   94-15585
[E]—dc20   CIP   AC

20 19 18 17 16   9/9 0/0

Printed in the U.S.A.   23

First Scholastic printing, November 1994

HICCUPS
for
Elephant

by James Preller
Illustrated by Hans Wilhelm

Hello Reader! — Level 2

SCHOLASTIC INC.
New York Toronto London Auckland Sydney

It was naptime.
All the animals were
fast asleep.

Except for Elephant.
He had the hiccups.

Chimp woke up.

"I can cure those hiccups,"
Chimp said.
"Stand on your head
and eat a banana."

Elephant gave it a try.

Ka-BOOM!
It only made him dizzy.

Lion woke up.

"I can cure those hiccups,"
Lion said.
"Drink lots of water
very, very fast."

Elephant gave it a try.

He drank
and drank
and drank
and drank.

Zebra woke up.

"I can cure those hiccups,"
Zebra said.
"Hold your breath and
count to 10 . . . backwards."

Elephant gave it a try.

10, 9, 8, 7, 6, 5, 4, 3, 2, 1—

Mouse woke up.

"What's all the noise?"
Mouse asked.
"I'm trying to sleep!"

"Poor Elephant has
the hiccups,"
Chimp explained.

Mouse looked Elephant
in the eye.
"BOO!" he shouted.

Everyone waited and waited.
But there were no more hiccups!

"Works every time,"
Mouse said.

All the animals
fell back to sleep.

Except for Elephant.